By Simon Crack

DEADCOOL

SPLATS By Simon Crack

Dedicated to my dad David Crack.
Special thanks to John Pryke.

Splark

(026. Bigius Bitius)

Eats everything.
Unfortunately allergic
to everything as well.

Dripfish

(101. Oh Cod)

A fish like creature that skips along the sea bed. It can speak fluent french.

Leggie

(002. Quick Step)

Extremely tall creature,
has an unfortunate
fear of heights.

Dripraffe

(003. Stretch Neck)

So tall it walks around with it's head in the clouds. Therefore thinks it's the only creature alive.

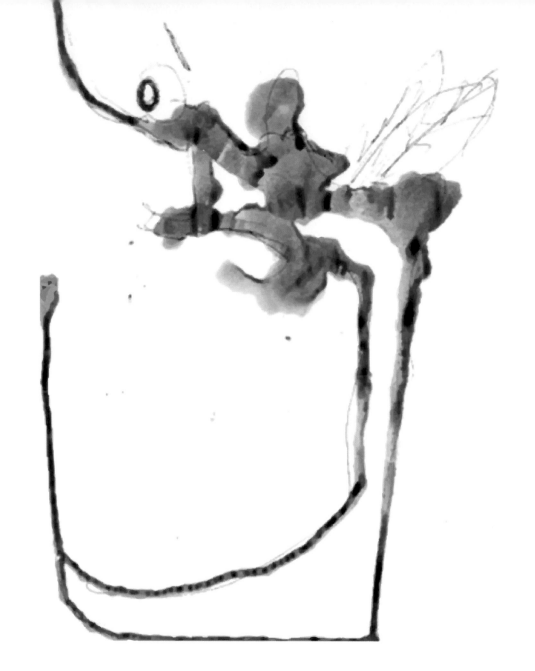

Mozy
(013. Buzz Buzz)

A shy, fly like creature. Has ski style legs, but prefers snowboarding.

Splooge

(087. Thinkalotus)

A very thoughtful creature. Always pondering the big questions, like what it should have for tea.

Splen

(007. Chick Chick)

Stands on one leg it's entire life.
No one knows quite why...

Bonce

(006. Justanoggin)

A kind creature, however only lives for a day due to the fact it's just a head.

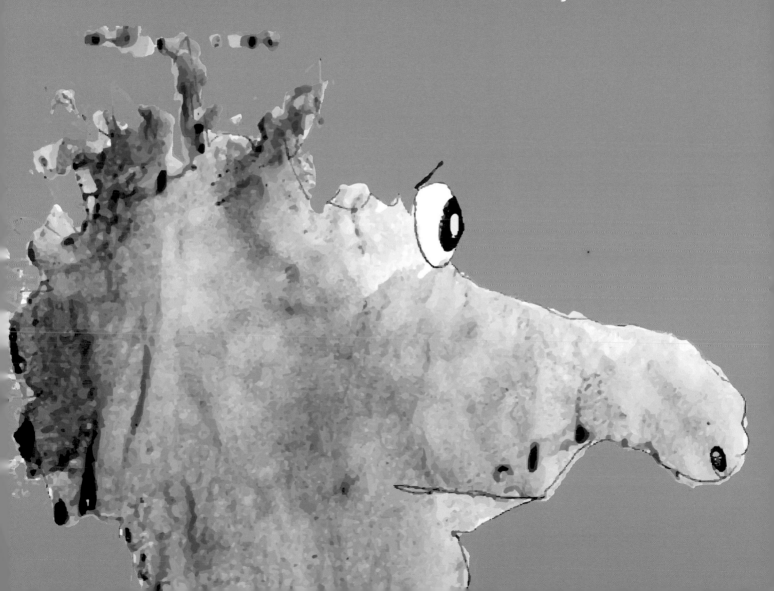

Splog

(023. K9)

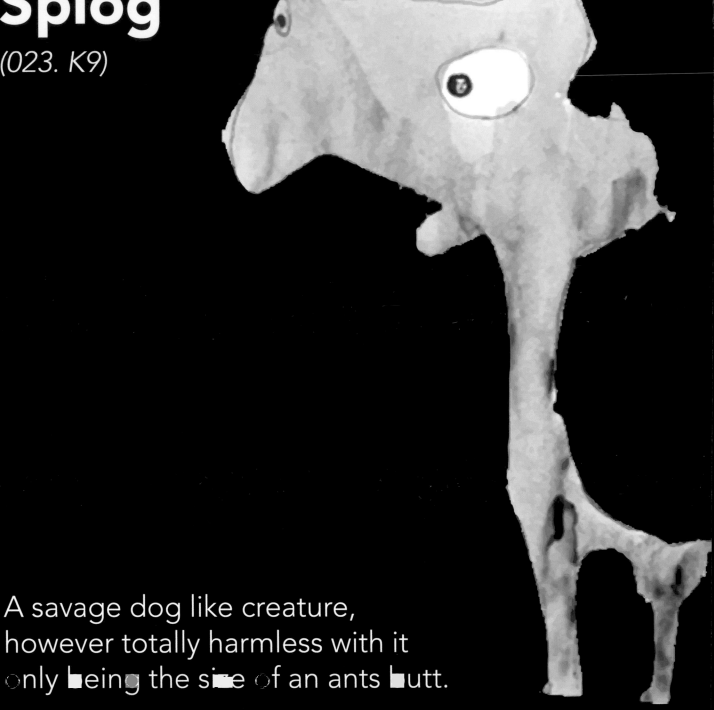

A savage dog like creature,
however totally harmless with it
only being the size of an ants butt.

Spake

(073. Not a Snakeius)

Found underwater but can't swim, so sits at the bottom of the sea bed.

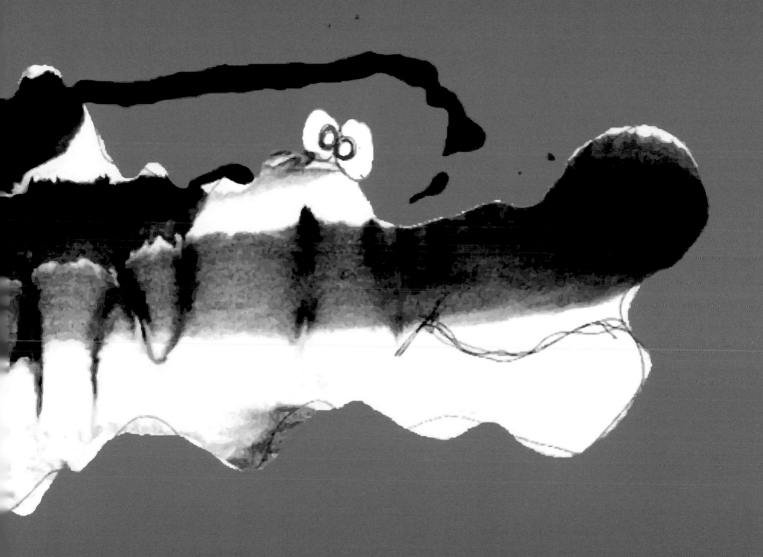

Fuzz

(048. Fluffy Stickius)

The smallest creature alive, it just looks bigger due to all it's fluff.

Twindo

(102. Two Birdius)

A two bird like
symbiotic creature.
The larger one
always gets
pooped on!

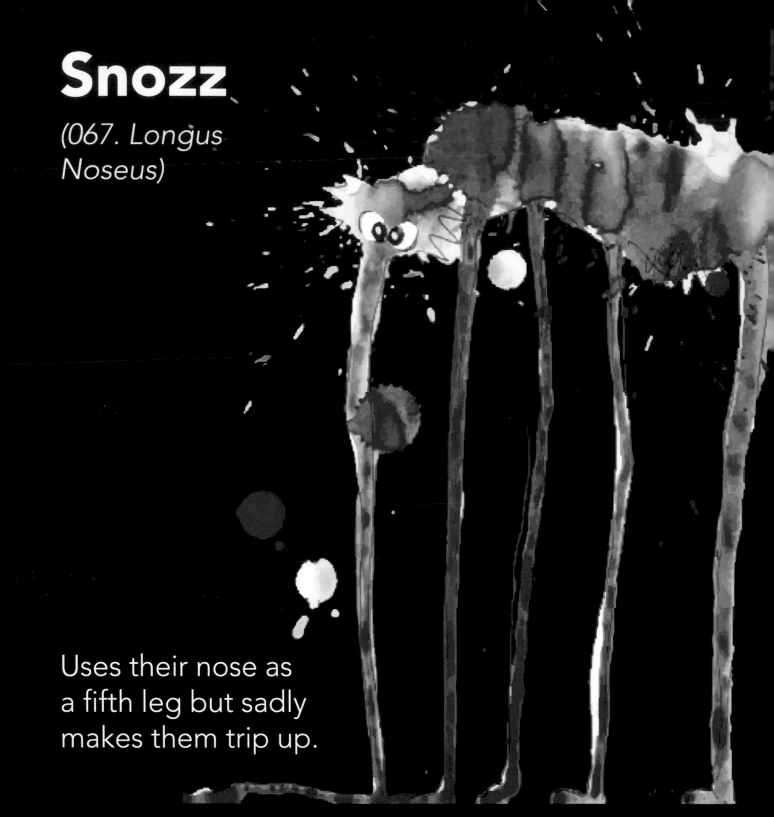

Snozz

(067. Longus Noseus)

Uses their nose as a fifth leg but sadly makes them trip up.

Splinker
(121. Wizius)

A very wise
creature, speak
to it for advice. It
won't hear you,
it has no ears.

Flutter Bye

(093. Twin Wing)

Creates lots of splat
mess when it flies,
aims for people!

Hog
Hedge

(005. Spikey)

Like a Hedgehog,
however the size
of a tick and
eats dogs...
hot dogs.

Crabby
(004. Crustius)

A crab like creature. Always shocked because it doesn't like water, but that's where it lives.

Old Bird

(014. Rag Tag)

A proud, tough
old bird, just
like my mum.

Name
- -
(Latin Name)
- -

Create
Your
Own!

Description
- -

- -

- -

Name

(Latin Name)

Description